Craft ILY EVER AFTER

#6

- -Breaking the Piggy Bank- -

By Martha Maker   Illustrated by Xindi Yan

LITTLE SIMON
New York London Toronto Sydney New Delhi

LITTLE SIMON

An imprint of Simon & Schuster Children's Publishing Division
1230 Avenue of the Americas, New York, New York 10020
First Little Simon hardcover edition January 2019
Copyright © 2019 by Simon & Schuster, Inc.
Jacket illustrations by Xindi Yan
Interior illustrations by Xindi Yan and Joy Yang
All rights reserved, including the right of reproduction in whole or in part in any form.
LITTLE SIMON is a registered trademark of Simon & Schuster, Inc., and associated colophon is a trademark of Simon & Schuster, Inc.
For information about special discounts for bulk purchases, please contact Simon & Schuster Special Sales at 1-866-506-1949 or business@simonandschuster.com.
The Simon & Schuster Speakers Bureau can bring authors to your live event. For more information or to book an event contact the Simon & Schuster Speakers Bureau at 1-866-248-3049 or visit our website at www.simonspeakers.com.
Designed by Laura Roode
The text of this book was set in Caecilia.
Manufactured in the United States of America 1218 FFG
2 4 6 8 10 9 7 5 3 1
Cataloging-in-Publication Data is available for this title from the Library of Congress.
ISBN 978-1-5344-2903-1 (hc)
ISBN 978-1-5344-2902-4 (pbk)
ISBN 978-1-5344-2904-8 (eBook)

CONTENTS

CHAPTER 1

Empty Shelves

It was *hot* out. And it was even hotter in the craft clubhouse, which was in Bella Diaz's backyard. Bella and her three best friends were there working on all sorts of different craft projects. They'd propped the doors open to catch the occasional breeze.

Despite the heat, the four friends were having fun. Sam Sharma was

pinning up his latest sketches and planning his next painting. Maddie Wilson was sewing sequins onto the sleeves of a dress she was making. Bella was writing code for a new video game. And Emily Adams had just finished sawing a piece of wood.

"Hey, are we out of sandpaper?" asked Emily after she checked the supply shelves.

Bella shrugged. "I don't usually use sandpaper when I'm coding." She laughed. "So I don't know. Are we out of it?"

"Looks like it. I need to sand

the puppy stepladder I'm making." Emily showed her new project to her friends. "See? Otherwise,
Woody will try to climb onto my
bed and end up with splinters in
all four paws!"

"Woof!" said Sam. "I guess we

need to pick up some sandpaper. In the meantime, want to grab a paintbrush and help me?"

"Sure," said Emily. But when she looked in the paint supply area, she called out, "We're out of paint, too."

"You guys can always sew with me," called Maddie. "Check it out! This is the dress I'm going to wear to my cousin's wedding!"

"Did you say *dress*?" asked Bella. "I think you mean shirt."

Sure enough, the garment looked way too short to be a dress!

"It's fine," said Maddie, rummaging through the sewing supplies. "I'll just piece together some more fabric and . . . Oh no! I thought we had plenty of this fabric. I can't go to the wedding with half a dress!"

"Want me to start a shopping list?" suggested Bella, opening a new window on her computer. "Paint, sandpaper, fabric . . . Anything else?"

"Yes," said Emily, looking at the craft clubhouse's mostly empty storage shelves. "We're running low on almost everything."

"What are we going to do?" asked Sam. "I can't paint without paint."

"And I can't sew without fabric," added Maddie.

"Yeah, wood might grow on trees, but sandpaper sure doesn't," joked Emily.

Bella laughed. "Well, how about we take a snack break and give ourselves some brain fuel," she suggested. "Then we can figure out how to get more supplies."

A Fresh Idea

"Yum," said Maddie, her mouth watering at the snacks Bella was assembling. "I wish my dad was a chef too."

"Is that pink lemonade?" asked Emily, spying a pitcher of what looked like her favorite drink.

"Not exactly. Try it," said Bella, pouring four cups.

"Wow," said Sam, draining his glass. "What is this? Watermelon juice?"

"Close. It's *agua fresca*," Bella explained. "It means 'fresh water,' and it's like Mexican lemonade, only with more fruit added. My dad's been perfecting new flavors for his restaurant. This one is watermelon-strawberry-basil.

What do you guys think?"

"Awesome," said Maddie. The others nodded and held out their cups for more.

"Hey, I have an idea!" said Emily. "Maybe we can earn money to restock our craft supplies by running a lemonade stand."

"Or an *agua fresca* stand," suggested Sam.

Everyone started talking excitedly at once. Carrying the snack tray, the cups, and the pitcher, they trooped back to the craft clubhouse and began planning.

"Luckily, we didn't run out of colored chalk!" said Maddie, wiping the chalkboard easel clean.

"And that's how we'll display our menu!" said Sam.

"When should we open for business?" asked Emily.

Bella pulled up the weather forecast on her computer. "This weekend?" she suggested, pointing to a sun under the word "Saturday."

"That's so soon," said Maddie. "Don't we need to figure out a recipe? And a location? And . . ."

"Whoa. Slow down!" Emily laughed. "That's why we're brainstorming right now."

On the chalkboard easel, she started a list:

-choose recipe
-get ingredients and supplies
-build a stand
-find chairs

"What else?" Emily asked.

"My mom says it's important to advertise," suggested Maddie, thinking of her mother's successful fashion-design and seamstress busi-ness.

"We could put up signs around the neighborhood," said Bella.

"Perfect!" Emily added Bella's suggestion to the list.

"And if we're trying to make money to get more supplies, then we're going to need somewhere to put all the money we earn . . . ," Sam said. "Like a super-cool piggy bank!"

"Totally!" Maddie agreed. "Because our *agua fresca* stand is going to be a hit!"

Everyone cheered as Emily added the suggestion to the list:

-make a piggy bank

This Little Piggy

Every afternoon that week, the four friends dashed over to Bella's to work on their preparations. With no paint, Sam decided to experiment with new sign-making materials. "Check this out," he told the others, leading them outside the clubhouse that Thursday.

The others gasped in surprise

when they saw Bella's walkway. The stone slabs, once plain and gray, was a rainbow of colors and designs.

Bella gasped the loudest. "Sam, what have you done? My parents didn't give us permission to paint the walkway!"

"It's not paint!" Sam sprayed some water to demonstrate. "I used chalk, so it comes right off. We could make some amazing signs for our stand this

way—on the sidewalks! And for walls and telephone poles, I made these."

He held up a red sign that said REFRESHING DRINKS! in yellow with a big green arrow.

"That's not paint either?" asked Maddie.

"Nope! Construction-paper collage!" said Sam proudly.

"So resourceful!" said Emily. "Speaking of which, come see what I've been doing."

Emily showed the others the stand . . . or what would soon be the stand. Right now it was two small bookcases and a bulletin

board. "See? I'm using some of my finished woodworking projects, all of which have already been sanded. It's sort of like a puzzle: Put them all together in the right way and we'll have a pretty fantastic lemonade—I mean *agua fresca*—stand."

"Nice!" said Bella. "Look at all those storage shelves for cups, spoons, napkins. . . ."

"And Mr. Oinkers!" said Maddie, holding up her project triumphantly.

"*Mr. Oinkers?*" asked Sam.

"That's his name," insisted Maddie. The bank did indeed look like a real pig. Maddie had given him eyes, ears, nostrils, and four empty thread spools for legs—even though the label on his side suggested that he had once been a mayonnaise jar.

"Is he hungry?" asked Bella. "Here you go, Mr. Oinkers!"

She produced a quarter from her pocket and "fed" it into the slot on his back.

"What's that you say, Mr. Oinkers?" said Maddie, holding the bank up to her ear and smiling. "You're still hungry? Just wait until Saturday. You'll get all the quarters, dimes, and nickels you want!"

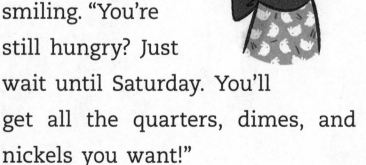

A Recipe for Success

The next afternoon, the four friends met at Bella's as usual. But this time they met in the kitchen instead of the clubhouse.

"It's time to perfect our recipe for success!" said Maddie.

"You mean our recipe for *agua fresca*," said Bella.

"Same thing!" replied Maddie

confidently. "According to my mom, a perfect product will sell itself."

"My dad always starts with the freshest fruit he can find," said Bella. "Sometimes melon, like we had the other day. Or tropical fruits, like guava or papaya. Or my favorite . . ."

Out of the fridge, Bella produced
a big basket of ripe red fruit.

"Ooh, strawberries!" the others
exclaimed excitedly.

Bella showed her friends a glass jar of clear liquid. "It's called simple syrup. Water and sugar cooked on the stove. My dad makes his own so it's ready for recipes whenever he needs it. And for the final touch—"

Bella plucked several sprigs off a plant on the windowsill.

"Fresh mint." She held the green leaves out for the others to sniff.

"Mmm!" they chorused. Bella popped the leaves into the blender with everything else and hit the on button.

Whirrrrr . . .

"Ahhh!"

In her excitement to show off her cooking skills, Bella had forgotten one important step: putting the lid on the blender.

The ceiling—and her friends—
were now covered with sticky
bright pink juice.

"Oh no!" wailed Bella. She ran
for the sink, tossing towels and
sponges in the direction of her
friends. "I'm so sorry! Look at the
mess I made!"

Sam peeked out from
under the towel that
had landed on his
head. He licked
his arm.

"Needs more
mint," he said.

Team Effort

On Saturday morning Maddie and Sam arrived at the craft clubhouse bright and early. Emily's family went to synagogue on Saturday mornings, so the four friends agreed not to open until she arrived.

Emily had hammered and glued the stand together in advance, but when Sam, Maddie, and Bella

attempted to move it to the sidewalk, they realized there was a
problem.

"Oof! This thing weighs a ton," said Sam.

"Let's try to lift it one more time," suggested Bella. "One, two . . . three!"

"*Errrrrrrr!*" The three friends grunted and groaned, but the stand stayed put.

"You guys don't think she accidentally glued the stand to the floor, do you?" asked Maddie.

"Emily wouldn't do that," insisted Sam. "Also, we're out of glue!"

"Okay, I have an idea," said Bella. She went inside and came back pushing a cart that looked like a ladder with wheels on the back and a platform at the bottom. "It's called a dolly. My dad uses it for bulk deliveries at the restaurant."

Together, the friends managed to wedge the bottom edge of the dolly under the bottom edge of the stand. Then they took several pieces of rope and secured it in place. And finally they all leaned on the stand until it shifted up and onto the dolly's wheeled platform.

"Quick, let's get it to the curb!" said Sam.

"Sam, go in front of me and clear a path," said Bella. "Maddie, help me steer!"

Soon the stand was in position on the sidewalk, with four chairs behind it and Maddie's hand-embroidered tablecloth disguising the bulletin-board top.

"Wow. It looks great!" said Emily, running up to join her friends. "Was it hard to move?"

"Noooooooooo," said the others, laughing.

"But when we finish," said Bella, "let's take it apart before we move it back to the clubhouse."

"No problem," said Emily. "Hey, are we ready to open? I told my parents they could be our first customers."

"I think so," said Bella, looking around. "A pitcher of *agua fresca*, a supply of cups, plenty of ice, napkins . . . I guess that's every-thing, right?"

"Almost!" said Maddie. "But we can't open without our most important team member." She held up the piggy bank.

"Mr. Oinkers!" cried Emily.

Just then Emily's mom and dad came strolling down the block.

"Places, everyone!" whispered Bella. "It's showtime!"

Yummy? Yucky? Yikes!

"Two cups of *agua fresca*, coming up!" said Emily after her parents placed their order. She poured the cups, accepted her parents' money, and unscrewed Mr. Oinkers's nose to make change.

"Keep the change," said her mom, making Emily and her friends beam. Then they watched expectantly as

Emily's mom and dad raised their cups to their lips.

"Oh my! It's . . . chunky, isn't it?" said Emily's mother, making an odd face.

"It's got real strawberries in it," said Bella. "Do you like it?"

"Oh yes," said Emily's father, chewing carefully. "It's very unusual. And . . . leafy." He picked a green bit

out of his front teeth. "I've never had anything quite like it. What did you say it's called?"

"*Agua fresca*," said Bella. "The flavor is strawberry-mint. Would you like some more? We've got plenty!"

"Oh, no, dear. This is perfect," said Emily's mom. "We should probably go. Good luck, kids! You've got the perfect day for a lemonade stand."

"*Agua fresca* stand," Emily corrected them.

After Emily's parents left, the four friends adjusted the tablecloth, positioned the pitcher and cups, and waited.

"I don't think your parents liked it," said Bella.

"Oh, no, they liked it," said Emily. "My mom loves lemonade. They probably just haven't had *agua fresca* before."

"Should we try it?" asked Sam. "I mean, just to make sure it tastes good."

"Of course it tastes good," said Bella. "It only has good stuff in it: strawberries, water, sugar, and fresh mint. Plus, if we drink it, there won't be enough for our customers."

"I guess you're right," said Sam, looking at the pitcher longingly.

The four friends waited. And waited some more.

"Where *is* everyone?" Maddie finally said.

"I don't know, but I am getting really hot out here," said Sam, wiping his brow with the back of his hand. "Are you sure we can't just have a teeny little sip?"

"I guess that would be all right," said Bella. "I'm pretty hot too."

She lined up four cups and poured a few sips' worth into each. The four friends gulped down the *agua fresca*—

And looked at one another.

"Oh no! Something's wrong!"
Bella cried, saying what everyone
else was thinking.

"Did you forget the sugar?" asked
Sam.

"I don't think so, but maybe I
used too little. That's not the big-
gest problem, though."

"I'll say!" said Emily. "It's much
too chunky!"

Bella felt embarrassed. She took the pitcher and marched over to her family's compost bin, ready to dump the dreadful drink.

"Wait!" yelled Maddie, running after her.

Back in Business?

"Don't throw it away!" Maddie said.

Bella shook her head. "My recipe is awful. Emily's parents would have spit it out if they weren't so nice!"

"It doesn't taste right *yet*," answered Maddie. "But maybe we can fix it. Doesn't your dad ever make mistakes in the kitchen?"

"I mean, yeah." Bella thought about all the times, even when she was a little kid in a booster chair, that her father offered a tasting spoon, then adjusted spices or added ingredients. Rarely did he start completely over. He just took whatever he had made and improved it.

"Maybe your dad can help us fix this," Maddie suggested.

"Great idea," Bella agreed.

So, while Emily and Sam watched the stand, Bella and Maddie went to consult Mr. Diaz. He took a taste, winced, then smiled.

"I made the same mistake the first time I made *agua fresca*," he told them.

Mr. Diaz got out a strainer and a big spoon, then showed Bella and Maddie how to strain the fruit chunks out of the drink and press them against the strainer with the spoon to squeeze every drop out.

"Try it now," he suggested.

"Hey, it's smooth," said Maddie. "And yummy!"

Bella closed her eyes and swirled the liquid around in her mouth. "It still needs a little more sugar. And a touch more mint," she added.

"That's my girl," said Mr. Diaz proudly.

Soon their concoction was perfect. Plus, Mr. Diaz helped them make a second batch, so now they had twice as much.

"You are now officially ready for the afternoon rush," said Mr. Diaz. "Go get 'em!"

The girls race-walked back to the stand, so as not to spill their pitchers.

At the stand they found Sam drawing with chalk and Emily reading a book.

"We're ready for business!" said Bella.

"With the tastiest *agua fresca* in history!" added Maddie.

"Great!" said Emily, putting her book away. "Now all we need is customers."

The four friends looked up and down the block. They could see Sam's colorful signs. But they didn't see a single person.

"Wait! There's someone!"

Sure enough, at the far end of the block, a woman was heading in their direction.

As she got closer, the four friends stood at attention behind the stand, politely waiting and hoping that she would stop. Finally, when the woman was still half a block away, Maddie couldn't stand it any longer.

"Excuse me!" Maddie called loudly. "Would you like to buy some *agua fresca*?"

The woman stopped right in front of the stand and seemed puzzled by the question. But then she took out her earbuds.

"Sorry? Some *what?*"

"*Agua fresca,*" Maddie repeated. "It's like lemonade but even more refreshing."

"Well, in that case, I should definitely try some," replied the woman, smiling.

As they had practiced, every-one took their positions. Maddie accepted the money and made change. Emily poured while Sam held the cup steady, and Bella offered a napkin.

They watched nervously as the woman took a sip. To their surprise, she quickly drained her glass.

"That," she said, "is the best *agua fresca* I have had in a very long time!"

"Wait. You know about *agua fresca*?" asked Bella.

"I know all about *agua fresca*," the woman said with a smile. "My name is Sofia Sanchez. I'm originally from Mexico City, so this reminds me of home! I'm on my way to work now, but I'd love a second cup before I go. I have a

radio show devoted to salsa music, and I DJ, too, so this will coat my vocal cords. It's so refreshing and *muy deliciosa!*"

"Really? You think it's delicious?" Bella was so excited.

"I do! But tell me . . . why don't you have a line of customers going all the way down the block?"

"We don't know!" admitted Sam. "I put signs up all over the neighborhood. And it's a hot day out. You'd think everyone would be outside."

"Not everyone enjoys the heat," said Sofia. "Some people prefer to sit inside with their fans and air conditioners on and read or listen to music . . . which gives me an idea!"

"What's your idea?" asked Bella.

"You'll see!" Sofia replied, finishing her second cup. "Or, rather, you'll *hear*," she added mysteriously before waving good-bye and continuing down the block.

A *Good* Problem

"Sam, we need more cups!" called Emily. "Bella?"

"I'm on it," called Sam, running out of Bella's house while balancing a tray of cups. He wasn't sure when the "afternoon rush" had kicked in, but—wow—had it ever! Bella was in the kitchen, mashing strawberries and straining more *agua fresca*. And

Maddie had emptied Mr. Oinkers twice to accommodate all the coins and bills.

"Thanks so much! Tell your friends," said Emily as another customer complimented her on how delicious the *agua fresca* was.

Just then Bella came out with a full pitcher in each hand.

"Great. Just in time!" said Maddie, taking payment from the next customer while Bella and Sam filled cups and Emily passed out paper fans to customers at the back of the line.

"Good thing I made those fans while we were waiting for business to pick up," said Emily, returning to the others.

"I know!" said Sam. "I guess people must be telling their friends

how good our *agua fresca* is."

"Actually, I heard about your stand on the radio," said a woman who had just bought three cups— one for herself and one for each of her two children.

"On the radio?"

"Sure! I was driving home from the pool when the DJ said she had just enjoyed the most refreshing summer treat. When she announced where your stand was located, I decided to come check it out."

"The DJ?" Bella and her friends said together in amazement.

"Yes, Sofia Sanchez," said the woman. "I love her salsa show."

Bella ran to get the radio from the craft clubhouse. She rigged up an extension cord long enough to reach the stand, then clicked it on.

"It sure is *hot* out there today," said a familiar voice. "So I'll be playing more hot salsa tunes in just a minute. One *cool* thing you can

do today is make a donation to our charity drive. We're raising money to buy winter clothing for those in need. Another cool thing you can do is try the most refreshing treat of the summer. It's available for a limited time, so get it while you can! Four wonderful young entrepreneurs and chefs are

running an *agua fresca* stand right now at the corner of . . ."

"Hey, that's us!" yelled Sam.

"Oh my gosh!" said Bella. So that's what Sofia had meant by "you'll hear"!

CHAPTER
9

Shopping Time!

"There you go," said Bella, pouring the last drop of *agua fresca* for a customer.

"Thank you!" said the man, handing over a bunch of coins.

"Thank *you*!" Sam flipped the OPEN sign he had made to CLOSED.

All four friends collapsed into their chairs.

"Wow. That was hard work," said Emily.

"It was," agreed Maddie. "But you guys, look!"

She dumped out Mr. Oinkers into the lockbox she had borrowed from her mom. His contents joined the bills and coins she had deposited there throughout the afternoon.

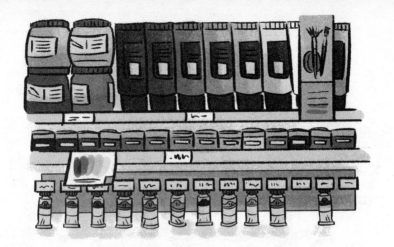

"Wow!" said Sam. "We're going to be able to restock every paint color in the rainbow."

"And every type of fabric and trim and buttons and thread," said Maddie.

"And wood and building supplies too," added Emily. "Hey, can we see how much a new hammer would cost? Oh, and we can't forget sandpaper. Lots and lots of sandpaper."

They started talking excitedly. Thinking about all the tools and supplies they could purchase gave them the energy they needed for the final cleanup. Together, they hauled bags of trash and recycling, disassembled the stand, and washed the dishes they'd used.

When they had cleaned everything up, they piled into Mrs. Diaz's car. They had to get to the bank before it closed so they could go shopping for supplies the next day.

At the bank the four friends held their collective breath as the machine gobbled up all their money and then reported the grand total.

"Wow!" said Emily. "That's twice as much as I thought it would be!"

"Hang on, you guys. Not all of that money is ours," Maddie pointed out. "Bella's parents bought all those berries and cups and napkins. We

need to pay them back first. The rest is our profit. That's the money we can use for whatever we want."

She got an envelope from the bank teller and set aside some money to repay Mrs. Diaz for the supplies.

Mrs. Diaz smiled at the kids. "All right, I'd better get you all home before dinnertime!" she said.

"And tomorrow," Bella said, "we shop!"

The next morning Mrs. Diaz picked everyone up from their homes. Together, they went to the hardware store, the art supplies store, the computer store, and the fabric shop. By the time they finished at the last store, the four friends had big bags to carry and even bigger

smiles. They jumped into the car, excited to be returning to the craft clubhouse with everything they needed to restock the shelves.

"Did you kids have fun?" Mrs. Diaz asked.

"Totally! I can't believe we were able to get all these crafting supplies," said Emily.

"I know. We got some great deals," agreed Maddie. "And we still have money left over!"

They piled back into the car. Mrs. Diaz switched on the radio as she started driving.

"We're about to start another hour of nonstop salsa," said a familiar voice. "But first I have a few community announcements."

"Hey, that's our friend Sofia Sanchez!" said Sam from the back seat.

"Your friend?" Mrs. Diaz looked surprised.

"Don't forget!" continued Sofia. "Our charity drive will close in one hour. As you know, a lot of families are in need of warm winter gear. Any donation makes a difference."

The whole car was silent for a moment as the DJ's words sank in. Then Emily piped up from the back seat.

"Are you guys thinking what I'm thinking?" she asked her friends.

Maddie and Sam nodded.

Bella turned to her mother. "Can we stop at the radio station on the way home? The one where Sofia Sanchez is a DJ?"

Mrs. Diaz looked at her daughter. Then she smiled. "Of course," she said.

Making a Difference

"Hello, salsa lovers! I have a very special treat this afternoon! Some of my fans have paid me a visit here at the radio station to bring in their donation in person. And you loyal listeners will recall that these are the very same kids you heard about yesterday. They raised this money through their own hard work. In fact, some of you may have visited their *agua fresca* stand based on my recommendation. Let me introduce to you Maddie, Emily, Sam, and Bella."

"Hi! Hello. Hey. *¡Hola!*" The four friends leaned into the microphone that Sofia Sanchez had set up for

them. Through the big window in the radio booth, Bella could see her mom beaming at them. And that made Bella feel extra good.

"I am pleased to report that, thanks to these four young people, we have made our fund-raising goal!

And I have an exciting announce-
ment: We have decided to extend
our deadline by one week! We're
hoping that even more of
our listeners, inspired
by the generosity these
kids have shown, will
join them. No donation
amount is too small
to make a difference!
And great things happen
when everyone pitches in. But I still
have one very important question
for my four new friends. Will you
promise to tell me when you have

your next *agua fresca* stand?"

"Of course!" Bella exclaimed.

"Perfect," said Sofia. "And I will make sure to tell all of you listening out there so you don't miss out on this *deliciosa* treat!"

Back at the craft clubhouse, the kids were almost done putting away all their new supplies. Sam had organized his paints in rainbow order. Emily had stored all her sandpaper in a portfolio, and then she'd even sorted her other supplies. Having made the *agua fresca* stand out of unusual materials, she wanted to make sure she could really see everything she had. Maybe next time she needed to make something, she could use unexpected materials again! Bella had also done

some cleaning up—she'd created files on the computer for each of the craft projects they'd done so far. And Maddie had rearranged her fabric by color and pattern and sorted her buttons and thread too.

"Whew!" Maddie said, falling back into the pile of pillows that made up their lounge area.

"Yeah, that was *a lot* of work," Emily agreed.

"I'm too tired to even *use* all my new paint colors," Sam said.

"Well," said Bella, "I think that leaves us with just one option. My dad experimented with some cookies called Mexican wedding cookies . . . and they're waiting for us in the kitchen."

The other three cheered.

"Maybe next time we'll have an *agua fresca* and cookie stand!" Emily said as they headed for the house.

"That's a good idea!" Bella said. "And we could add some more counter space to the stand to make room."

"And I could make flyers to hand out at school, and then we could donate all the money we make to Sofia's charity."

"I think we're going to need a few more of Mr. Oinkers for the next *agua fresca* stand!" Maddie exclaimed.

The kids laughed and chattered about their ideas as they went inside for their hard-earned snacks!

How to Make . . .
A Bottle Bank

What you need:

Empty bottle
Construction paper
Scissors
Double-sided tape
Glue
4 empty spools of thread
Dish soap

Step 1: Find an empty bottle and rinse it out with soap and water. Let it dry.

Step 2: Turn the bottle sideways. Cut a slot on the top side of the bottle for coins.

Step 3: Out of construction paper, cut eyes, ears, and nostrils. The ears should have tabs at the bottom so they're easy to tape down.

Step 4:

Attach the eyes, ears, and nostrils with double-sided tape.

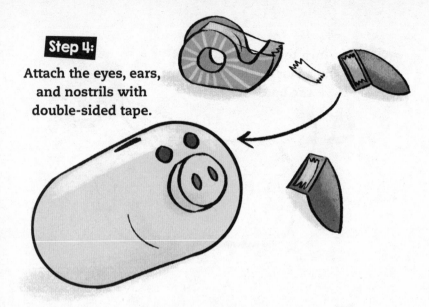

Step 5: You can decorate the "body" with more construction paper as well. Use double-sided tape to secure everything.

Step 6: Attach the spools of thread using glue. These are the legs.

Oink! Oink! You're done!

If you like Craftily Ever After, then you'll love . . .

the adventures of
SOPHIE MOUSE

EBOOK EDITIONS ALSO AVAILABLE
from LITTLE SIMON
simonandschuster.com/kids

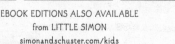